THE WIND IN THE WILLOWS

by KENNETH GRAHAME

#3 The Wild Wood

Adapted by Laura Driscoll

Illustrated by Ann Iosa

Sterling Publishing Co., Inc.

New York

Library of Congress Cataloging-in-Publication Data Available

10   9   8   7   6   5   4   3

Published 2007 by Sterling Publishing Co., Inc.
387 Park Avenue South, New York, NY 10016
Originally published and copyright © 2004 by Barnes and Noble, Inc.
Illustrations © 2004 by Ann Iosa
Distributed in Canada by Sterling Publishing
$^{c}/_{o}$ Canadian Manda Group, 165 Dufferin Street
Toronto, Ontario, Canada M6K 3H6
Distributed in the United Kingdom by GMC Distribution Services
Castle Place, 166 High Street, Lewes, East Sussex, England BN7 1XU
Distributed in Australia by Capricorn Link (Australia) Pty. Ltd.
P.O. Box 704, Windsor, NSW 2756, Australia

Printed in China   12/09

Sterling ISBN-13: 978-1-4027-3295-9
       ISBN-10: 1-4027-3295-3

For information about custom editions, special sales, premium and
corporate purchases, please contact Sterling Special Sales
Department at 800-805-5489 or specialsales@sterlingpub.com.

Contents

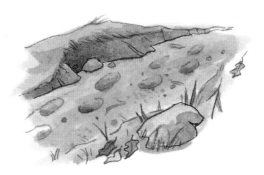

Noises

Mole wanted to visit
Mr. Badger in the Wild Wood.
Mole had never met Badger
and he had never been
in the Wild Wood.

"Badger is shy,"
Rat said.
"Let us wait for him
to come see us.

Mole could not wait.
One winter day,
while Rat was napping,
Mole sneaked away.
He set off alone
into the Wild Wood.

At first, Mole was having fun.

He was having an adventure!

Then Mole noticed
it was very quiet.
And—*eek!*
Inside a hole,
Mole thought he saw
a face watching him.
Then he saw another,
then another!

It was getting dark.

Mole walked faster.

He heard a whistle

behind him.

He heard a whistle

in front of him.

Then Mole heard
the *pat-pat-pat* of feet.
It was all around him!

Mole began to run.

Mole saw a hollow in a tree.
He ran inside to hide.
Mole did not think
he liked the Wild Wood
very much at all.

Lost and Found

Back at home,
Rat woke up
from his nap.
He could not find Mole.
Rat opened the door.
He saw Mole's tracks.
He saw they led to
the Wild Wood.
"Oh, dear," Rat said.
"I must find Mole!"

So Rat set off
into the Wild Wood.
"Moly!" he called.
"Where are you?"

Soon Rat heard a voice,
a very small voice.
"Ratty," it said.
It came from the
hollow of a tree.
Rat crept inside,
and there was Mole!
"Oh, Rat," said Mole.
"I've been so scared!"

"I know, Mole," said Rat.
"The Wild Wood can be
a scary place—
if you're all alone.
But I'm here now."

Mole felt better
with Rat there.
But he was so tired!
So Mole took a nap
while Rat stood guard.

Snow!

When Mole woke up
he and Rat got ready
to start home.
Rat peeked outside.
"Oh, my!" Rat said.

Mole peeked outside, too.

It was snowing.

It was snowing hard!

Now the woods looked
very different.
Everything was white.

It was hard for Rat
to find his way.
He tried and tried,
but soon…

Rat and Mole were lost!

They looked around
for a place to rest.
But then—*oof!*
Mole tripped over something.
"Ouch!" said Mole.

Rat dug in the snow
to see what Mole tripped over.
Soon he found a broom.

And that's not all....

Rat dug some more.

Soon he found a doormat.

And that's not all....

Rat dug some more.

Mole dug, too.

Do you know
what they found?

It was a door.

It was the door
to Mr. Badger's house!

Mr. Badger

Mole rang the doorbell.
Rat knocked.
They heard footsteps
behind the door.

The door opened a crack.
A long, striped nose and
sleepy eyes peeked out.
"Who is it?" asked a grumpy voice.

"Badger!" said Rat.
"It's me, Rat,
and my friend Mole.
We've lost our way
in the snow!"

"Why, Ratty!" cried Badger.
Now his voice was friendly.
The door flew open.
"Come in, both of you!"